Berkeley's
BARN OWL DANCE

With love to Kim, M&D, P&M and our owlets, Kylan, Truce and Evey.
And heartfelt thanks to Yvette Ghione and KCP for giving a hoot! — T.J.

For my dad, who taught me all about the love of birds — T.H.

Kids Can Press acknowledges the financial support of the Government of Ontario, through the Ontario Media Development Corporation's Ontario Book Initiative; the Ontario Arts Council; the Canada Council for the Arts; and the Government of Canada, through the BPIDP, for our publishing activity.

Published in Canada by
Kids Can Press Ltd.
29 Birch Avenue
Toronto, ON M4V 1E2

Published in the U.S. by
Kids Can Press Ltd.
2250 Military Road
Tonawanda, NY 14150

www.kidscanpress.com

The art in this book was rendered digitally.
The text is set in Alghera.

Edited by Yvette Ghione
Designed by Karen Powers
Printed and bound in Singapore

This book is smyth sewn casebound.

The paper used to print this book was produced with elemental chlorine-free pulp, harvested from managed sustainable forests.

CM 08 0 9 8 7 6 5 4 3 2 1

Library and Archives Canada Cataloguing in Publication

Johnson, Tera
    Berkeley's barn owl dance / written by Tera Johnson ; illustrated by Tania Howells.

ISBN 978-1-55453-263-6

1. Barn owl—Juvenile fiction. I. Howells, Tania II. Title.

PS8619.O484B47 2008   jC813'.6   C2007-906614-3

Kids Can Press is a *l'orus*™ Entertainment company

Berkeley's
BARN OWL DANCE

written by Tera Johnson

illustrated by Tania Howells

KIDS CAN PRESS

Berkeley Barn Owl loved to dance, and any occasion would do. She fluffed her stuff for hatchings and moltings and even first flights, under the spotlight moon.

But tonight wasn't just any occasion. The
Leave the Nest Fall Fest was the biggest barn owl
dance of the year. Next evening, Berkeley would
be leaving with her fellow fledglings, Bo and Bree.

Berkeley   Bo   Bree

With flapping wings and tapping talons, she wowed the crowd. The faster the clapping, the faster she flapped.

The louder the clapping, the louder she tapped. Berkeley Barn Owl was a hoot!

When at last the fading moon said good morning, the three fledglings flopped into their nest. Even Berkeley couldn't dance all day. They nestled in tight and waited for night in the safe, warm barn.

The next moonrise, Bo and Bree were already
stretching their wings when Berkeley peeked outside.
She shrieked as only young barn owls can. "I don't
want to go," she cried, scrunching into the corner
and scattering pellets everywhere.

Poppa Owl puffed his ruff and
smoothed Berkeley's feathers. "You are
ready for your own barn, my owlet.
Your dance is just beginning."

Berkeley turned wide eyes on Momma Owl.
"What will I do when I'm all alone?" she asked.

Momma Owl swaddled Berkeley in her wings.
"You will eat and sleep, fly and preen, and in
between, you will dance."

"Will you visit me?" Berkeley asked in a
downy whisper.

"Of course," her parents twittered.

"And you'll come back every year for
the Leave the Nest Fall Fest," said Poppa Owl.
"You will share your story and teach the fledglings
to dance before they spread their own wings."

From below they heard clapping, and together they looked down on a great good-bye gathering. With a feathertip tap from Momma Owl, Berkeley curtsied and took up the dance. FLAPPITY, TAPPITY, CLAP CLAP CLAP. FLAPPITY, TAPPITY, FLAP FLAP FLAP!

Then, with hugs and kisses and farewell wishes, Berkeley, Bo and Bree flew after the shape-shifting moon.

That night, the winking moon said,
"Follow me into the valley. You will find
a wood filled with bats and birds."

And a few nights and thousands of silent
wingbeats later, Berkeley, Bo and Bree did.

Flappity, tappity, clap clap clap. Flappity,
tappity, flap flap FLOP ... Berkeley started a
tree dance, but the wind knocked her off her
branch. "A tree just isn't as safe as a barn,"
thought Berkeley.

So she and Bo nestled in tight and
waited for night in the singing wood.

A wide-awake Bree bounced from branch to branch. When she hopped to the top of the tree, she dug in her talons, spread her wings and waved at the windy world below. And by the end of the day, Bree had decided to stay.

That night, the smiling
moon said, "Follow me through
the wood. You will find a bridge over
a stream filled with fish and frogs."
And a few nights and thousands
of silent wingbeats later, Berkeley
and Bo did.

Flappity, tappity, clap clap CLOP ...
Berkeley began a bridge dance, but her
wings got cold and wet. "A bridge just isn't
as warm as a barn," thought Berkeley.

So she nestled in tight and waited for
night above the burbling stream.

A wide-awake Bo bounced
from beam to beam. When he
swooped to the surface of the
stream, he dangled his talons,
stretched his wings and waved at
the watery world below. And by the
end of the day, Bo had decided to stay.

That night, the laughing moon said,
"Follow me along the stream. You will find
a farm filled with bats and birds, fish and
frogs, and mice and voles."

And a few nights and thousands
of silent wingbeats later, all on
her own, Berkeley did.

"A safe, warm barn!" shrieked Berkeley, landing in a flurry of feathers.

"You-hooooo," she called into the
dark. But no owl replied.

As Berkeley peered into the barn
she bumped a loose shingle, and the
merry moon peeked in.

Suddenly the barn was filled with a chorus of baas, meows, neighs, woofs, peeps, clucks and oinks! All of the animals were awake in the middle of the night, and no one knew what to do.

oink!

cluck!

meow!

peep!

But Berkeley did. It was a barn, after all! She curtsied to the crowd like Momma Owl, puffed her ruff like Poppa Owl, and fluffed her stuff like only she knew how.

FLAPPITY, TAPPITY, CLAP CLAP CLAP.
FLAPPITY, TAPPITY, FLAP FLAP FLAP!

The animals stopped to gawk at
Berkeley's midnight show.

"Helloooo," she sang. "I'm Berkeley
Barn Owl, and I love to dance! Whooo'll
join me?" Her voice echoed in the quiet.

Then a hen in the hayloft
started to flappity.

And a cat in the
corner started to tappity.

Soon all the animals joined in with a CLAP CLAP CLAP!
From high in the rafters, a young barn owl gave a hoot.
"Helloooo," he said with waggling wings. "I'm Oliver, and I'd
love to join you, too, Berkeley."

So with flapping wings and tapping talons, and claws and hooves and paws, too, Berkeley's new dance began, under the spotlight moon.